TABLE OF CONTENTS

HUNTING DOGS **6**

COMPANIONS **8**

SLED DOGS **10**

TERRIERS **12**

RACING DOGS **14**

SHEEPDOGS **16**

WORKING DOGS **18**

BITCHES AND THEIR PUPPIES **20**

DOG POSTURES **22**

TRAINING YOUR DOG **24**

TAKING CARE OF YOUR DOG **26**

OUR ANIMAL WORLD IN PICTURES

DOGS

AN INTRODUCTION FOR CHILDREN FROM 6 TO 10

Conception
Émilie BEAUMONT

Images
Lindsey SELLEY

Translation
Lara M. ANDAHAZY

FLEURUS

HUNTING DOGS

There are basically two different kinds of hunting dogs—hounds and pointers. Hounds run after the game and are able to track it by smell. In the old days they took part in large stag hunts. We get the expression to hound someone from their name. Pointers are ideal companions for solitary hunters. Their job is to flush out the game on their masters' orders and then retrieve it once it is shot. A good pointer carries the game carefully in its mouth so as not to damage it.

Brittany Spaniels

These are the most popular of all French pointers. Brittany spaniels are kind and affectionate. They do a wonderful job finding birds such as pheasants and woodcocks. You can recognize them by their brown and white spotted fur and short tails.

German Shorthaired Pointers

These dogs (above) are a perfect example of a pointer. As soon as they smell the game they freeze, standing still with their tails stretched out horizontally and one front paw lifted up, their noses pointed in the direction of the game. They wait for their masters to give the order to flush out the game.

A Hound—the Beagle

Beagles are ideal when it comes to finding game and can even pick up its scent several hours after the animal has gone by. They are small, short-haired dogs but are difficult to train. When hunting season is over they make excellent guard dogs.

Irish Setters

The Irish setter to the left has just retrieved the pheasant that its master shot. Irish setters are a kind of pointer. They are able to retrieve game killed in hard to reach areas.

COMPANIONS

In the past we used to choose dogs based on the kind of work we wanted them to do for us such as keep guard, hunt, watch over sheep, pull sleds, etc. Nowadays we choose dogs for their looks, their characters and the happiness they can bring us. But you have to think carefully before buying a dog because they are not toys to be left in a corner or abandoned on a street corner. Dogs need lots of care and company. You need to keep in mind where he will live when you choose your dog.

Chihuahuas are the tiniest of all dogs. They are not always nice to strangers.

Pekinese have a bad reputation as lazy and spoiled dogs. All the same, they are very playful animals. Their eyes need regular care.

The shar-pei is the most expensive dog of all. They are covered in wrinkles. Can you find the shar-pei on the cover?

Poodles are easy to live with, very smart and playful. The poodle below is wearing the "English Saddle" clip that needs lots of upkeep.

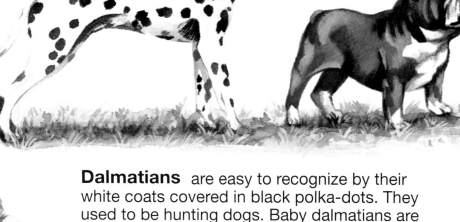

Dalmatians are easy to recognize by their white coats covered in black polka-dots. They used to be hunting dogs. Baby dalmatians are all white when they are born. Their spots appear after they are weaned.

French bulldogs are affectionate and very gentle even though they are often scary looking.

Yorkshire terriers (left and below) are small dogs with lots of personality. They are gentle and love to be petted. They need lots of looking after because their long fur needs to be brushed every day. They are very sensitive and are unhappy if you are too rough with them. They make good friends for children. Their only flaw is that they bark a lot.

Maltese dogs have calm natures and love comfy cushions! They are intelligent but can be aggressive with strangers. Their long fur needs lots of care, especially if you want to enter them in beauty contests.

SLED DOGS

For generations, the Eskimos that live in the great white north were nomads. They needed resistant animals to move about. After much crossbreeding they obtained sled dogs. Sled dogs are able to pull heavy weights across long distances in difficult climactic conditions. They are sometimes replaced by snowmobiles but these dogs are still the surest way to move across ground covered in snow and ice.

Sled Team Formation

The lead dog is placed at the front. He is the smartest and most docile of the pack. The lead dog leads the team and obeys his master's voice. The strongest dog in the pack is placed at the back—he's the boss in charge of keeping an eye on all the others. After work, sled dogs need to eat and rest. They have hearty appetites.

Warm and Snug in the Snow

At night these dogs curl up in balls with their tails wrapped snugly around themselves. They can stand the coldest weather (sometimes as much as −75°F!) because their thick, long-haired fur coats keep them warm.

Siberian Huskies

The Siberian husky is the best-known sled dog. They have slightly almond-shaped blue eyes rimmed in black. They are fast and robust dogs.

Tiny Boots for Their Paws

At the end of the day, the dogs' master examines them carefully. If the dogs' feet are hurt he will protect them from the cold with tiny boots. These boots are made out of shark skin or knitted wool and attached to the paws with a leather lace or piece of string. The dogs also wear these tiny boots to protect their paws when they have to cross stretches of rough ice.

11

TERRIERS

Terriers were originally farmers' hunting dogs. They were trained to catch foxes which they would follow all the way to the bottom of their dens (called earths). Today they have become house dogs but they have not lost their hunting instincts. If they go to the countryside and the scent of a rabbit or fox makes their whiskers twitch they'll be off in a flash chasing after it. When they come back they are often covered in dirt and in need of a good bath.

Aren't these wire-haired terrier puppies adorable? They look like balls of fluff. They will look like their mother only after their fur has been clipped for the first time.

Scottish terriers come from Scotland as their name suggests. They are especially good at catching badgers and weasels in their dens.

Scottish Terrier

Bull Terrier

Smooth-coated Dachshund

Bull terriers are very affectionate with children but they love to fight. They used to be used in bullfights. **Smooth-coated dachshunds** are often called "sausage dogs." These small dogs are ideal for visiting dens. They have strong personalities. Dachshunds do not like cold and humidity.

Fox Terriers Are Quarrelsome

There are two types of fox terriers— wire-haired (pictured below with her puppies) and smooth-haired fox terriers (above). The second was the first terrier of all. These dogs are affectionate and playful. Their flaws are that they are quarrelsome and often ready to attack other dogs. Careful! Their teeth are formidable. Wire-haired fox terriers tend to run off. You have to keep a close watch on them because they are perfectly capable of rushing off right under your nose. You can call and call but they won't listen! They'll come back when they are good and ready!

Airedale Terriers

These dogs are larger than fox terriers but look a bit like them. Airedale terriers are brown with black backs. They have always been seen as the king of the terriers. They are easy to live with, very smart and love water.

Wire-haired fox terriers need to have their coats clipped regularly to keep their characteristic look. Otherwise, they quickly look like small, curly-haired sheep.

13

RACING DOGS

Greyhounds and other racing dogs are among the oldest dogs; the first greyhounds go back to around 5000 B.C.. They are agile and noble looking dogs that used to belong to noble and wealthy families and were used in hunting. Greyhounds are very elegant dogs with their long legs and svelte bodies. They are excellent runners and their owners have to run them often and lots. They are not easy to take for walks because they have a tendency to attack other dogs.

Borzois

Borzois (also called Russian wolfhounds) are among the most handsome racing dogs but they are not easy to raise. They need lots of exercise and their health is delicate.

A Hunting Dog

Greyhounds are used as hunting dogs in some countries. They can catch a hare without any problem after seeing it from afar because they can run so quickly.

Salukis

Salukis are said to have been the first domestic dogs. In the past they were used in deserts to hunt gazelles because they can run at speeds of over 37 miles per hour.

Greyhounds Are Aggressive

Greyhounds (pictured above and left) are difficult to take for walks because they attack other dogs. They need to be kept on leashes. They are required to wear muzzles in many cities.

Dog Races

Dog races are very popular in England. The greyhound is the most commonly used dog. Racing greyhounds are trained very young and stop running when they are about four years old. In dog races they are made to chase after a live hare or a decoy (the dogs are made to think that they are running after a live hare when it is really just a fake one). They run between about 900 and 1,500 feet.

SHEEPDOGS

Sheepdogs used to be trained to protect the flocks from wild beasts like bears and wolves. Nowadays their main job is to watch over the animals in order to make sure that none of them get lost. Each country "created" its own ideal sheepdog based on what kind of work it wanted the dog to do. Many races of sheepdogs are named after the countries that they originally come from, for example the Old English sheepdog, the German shepherd and the Belgian sheepdog, etc.

Belgian Cattle Dogs

Belgian cattle dogs are also called Bouvier des Flandres and come from Belgium. They are good guardians and are mostly used to look after herds of cows. They are quick to nip at the legs of cows that don't obey fast enough.

Old English Sheepdogs

Old English sheepdogs (above) are also called "bob-tails." They watch after sheep in English meadows. They have lots of long fur and are often clipped at the same time as the sheep. They make very gentle pets and love children.

Border Collies

Border collies are also excellent guardians and keep one eye on the sheep and one eye on their masters so as not to miss any orders. They are lively and authoritarian and love exercise. They are not the best dogs to have in an apartment.

Briards

Big dogs, Briards are typical French sheepdogs. They have long fur that hangs in their faces and hides their eyes, but that doesn't make it hard for them to see. And not a single sheep can escape their watchful eyes!

WORKING DOGS

Some dogs are raised to do specific jobs, for example labradors are very often trained as guide dogs for the blind. German shepherds are very often trained for difficult tasks such as finding people trapped under rubble, helping in mountain rescue missions, detecting the presence of drugs in cars and airplanes and so on. All working dogs begin their training at a very young age. Their training courses are very intensive and both the dogs and their masters follow them.

Guide Dogs for the Blind (right)

Guide dogs start their training with a specialist when they are about two months old. Their training lasts until they are one year old. Labradors, especially females, are very often trained as guide dogs. They work as guide dogs only when wearing their harness and can direct their masters, help them avoid obstacles and let them know when to stop, etc. The dogs' masters have to trust them completely.

Rescue Dogs

After earthquakes or avalanches, rescue dogs are used to help find the victims trapped under the rubble or snow. These dogs are able to follow difficult paths once they have picked up the scent of the victim who is trapped. They are always accompanied by their masters who have to be able to follow them anywhere.

Training Rescue Dogs

Rescue dogs first learn how to find their masters hidden alone and then hidden with another person; finally, they have to be able to find a stranger hidden alone with a "toy." Finding someone is a game for these dogs and they do not really need to smell a piece of clothing that belonged to the missing person to find them.

Police Dogs

These dogs, usually German shepherds, are trained to attack on command and stop criminals from running away or attacking. They can also be used by the police or the army to locate explosives or drugs very quickly. In the picture above the dog is searching a car for drugs. The dog's keen sense of smell lets it find the drugs without our having to take the car apart.

BITCHES AND THEIR PUPPIES

Right after her puppies are born, the mother dog licks vigorously all over to clean them and help them breathe. Puppies can't see or hear when they are first born. They stay snuggled close to their mother because they need to keep warm. Puppies spend most of their time sleeping or nursing. Most of the time dogs give birth without any problem and don't need any help. However, you need to watch over the birth when the mother is a very small dog.

Unlike many other baby animals such as cats, puppies suckle any of their mother's teats without having a favorite place. This way, the puppies don't get into fights at feeding time.

20

Prepare a Bed for the Puppies

When your dog is going to have puppies it is best to make a bed for her in a box or basket lined in soft cloth and placed in a dark spot where it is not too cold. Like most animals, she needs to have "her nest" where she feels at home to give birth to her babies.

A Puppy's Life

During the first days of their lives, puppies sleep a lot. They open their eyes and start to move about more in the second week. When they are one month old they can see very well and hear. They start to eat more than just their mothers' milk. They also play a lot with their brothers and sisters.

How to Carry Your Puppy

There is nothing nicer than carrying an adorable puppy in your arms. But watch out! You have to be careful about how you pick up a puppy. You have to support the weight of its whole body and never pick up a puppy by holding it under its front legs alone.

DOG POSTURES

We often say, "If only dogs could talk!" but they don't need words to make themselves understood. You can tell if a dog wants to play or is getting ready to bite by looking at the position of its body, how it is holding its ears and the movement of its tail and by listening to the sound of its bark. On the other hand, we still don't know why in certain circumstances a dog will start howling very loudly. They sometimes do this when they hear church bells.

Come and Play

In order to ask a smaller dog to play with him, a big dog will lay down on its back with its back legs spread apart. This is to show his good intentions. If the little dog

Ready to Bite

When a dog's body is tense, its ears pulled back and it shows its teeth while growling and barking, it is defending its territory against a strange person or another dog. If its master doesn't calm him down he could very easily bite.

doesn't come play, the big dog will try to get its attention by jumping about. When dogs wants to play with their masters, they often go get their ball or bone and place it at their masters' feet. Then they start to bark joyfully with their hind ends in the air and their front legs bent while wagging their tails at top speed.

A Frightened Dog

When a dog has got into mischief and is scolded by its master, it puts its tail between its legs, lowers its hind end and moves slowly. Sometimes a dog will even crawl with its head and tail down and its ears flattened against its head in reaction to an angry look from its master.

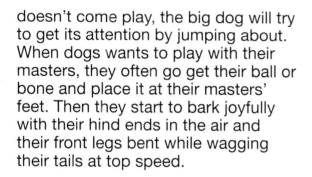

TRAINING YOUR DOG

You have to start training your dog at a very young age otherwise he will quickly pick up bad habits that can cause big problems for your family.
For example, if you let the dog you adopt bark at just about anything, your neighbors will most likely get upset; and if your dog goes potty on the living room rug instead of outside or if he regularly eats your shoes or curtains, life won't be any fun at all!

Old English Sheepdog (Can you find the picture of the Old English sheepdog on the cover?)

You should take your dog for its walks on a leash from the very beginning. (This is the law in many cities.) You should quickly get him used to walking at the same speed as you and teach him not to pull against the leash.

Toilet Training

Puppies often go potty soon after eating or when they first wake up. So that your puppy doesn't go potty just anywhere you can train it to go on a newspaper by putting it on it when he has to go potty. You can also train it to go potty outside by carrying him out when it is time.

Reward and Punishment

When your dog obeys an order you have to reward him right away by petting him or giving him a treat. This way he will start to understand and continue to obey. If he does something bad you have to punish him right away. It isn't good to punish him when you get home in the evening for eating your shoes earlier in the day because he won't understand. He is happy to see you and isn't able to understand the link between the punishment and the bad deed because too much time has passed between the two.

Obeying Orders

Your dog should learn to obey a few basic orders such as "stay," "come," "heel" and "sit." To teach him how to sit for example you push gently on his rear end to make him sit while saying "sit." Little by little your puppy will learn to associate the word "sit" with the proper position.

TAKING CARE OF YOUR DOG

If you adopt a dog that you find, you need to take him to see a veterinarian for a thorough check-up. The vet will also give you advice on how best to feed him. If you buy a puppy in a pet store be sure to ask about his medical history. You have to make sure that your new pet has had all the right vaccinations before letting him outside. Sometimes a change in his feeding can upset his stomach for a little while.

Advice on Bathing

Your dog should have his first bath when he is about four months old (after he has been vaccinated). It is best to brush his coat to get out any knots before you give him his bath. The water should be lukewarm and it is easier to give him a bath with a movable shower head. You should start shampooing him at the back and move forward to end with his head.

Cocker Spaniel

For a good, healthy dog you need to feed him a varied diet at regular hours and take him out several times a day for exercise. Above all, don't forget the booster shots for his vaccinations (especially rabies vaccinations).

Brushing your dog's fur regularly lets you keep an eye on the condition of his skin and watch out for fleas and other dangerous parasites like ticks. Some dogs such as poodles and fox terriers need to be clipped from time to time by a professional.

Caring for His Teeth

Your dog's teeth need to be examined regularly and, when needed, polished by a vet. Giving your dog a bone to chew on can help prevent cavities.

Be very careful not to get soap in his eyes and ears. After he shakes himself you can dry him off with a towel and a hair-dryer set on cool.

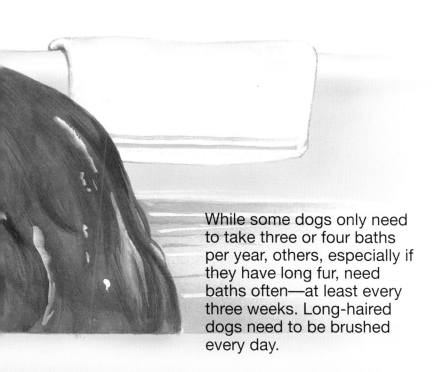

While some dogs only need to take three or four baths per year, others, especially if they have long fur, need baths often—at least every three weeks. Long-haired dogs need to be brushed every day.

Caring for His Ears

You need to look in your dog's ears from time to time and clean them with a soft cloth when they get dirty. If your dog scratches his ears too often he needs to see a vet because he might have an ear infection or be bothered by something caught in his ears.

ISBN 2-215-06166-9

Printed in Italy.